SPACE PATROL

BY JULIUS GOODMAN

ILLUSTRATED BY RALPH REESE

An R.A. Montgomery Book

BANTAM BOOKS
TORONTO · NEW YORK · LONDON · SYDNEY

RL 4, IL age 10 and up

SPACE PATROL

A Bantam Book / July 1983

CHOOSE YOUR OWN ADVENTURE ® is a registered trademark of Bantam Books, Inc. Registered in U.S. Patent and Trademark Office and elsewhere.

Original conception of Edward Packard

ISBN 0-553-23349-1

Published simultaneously in the United States and Canada

Bantam Books are published by Bantam Books, Inc. Its trademark, consisting of the words "Bantam Books" and the portrayal of a rooster, is Registered in U.S. Patent and Trademark Office and in other countries. Marca Registrada. Bantam Books, Inc., 666 Fifth Avenue, New York, New York 10103.

PRINTED IN THE UNITED STATES OF AMERICA

O   0 9 8 7 6 5 4 3 2 1

To Kate and Ray

with special thanks to
all space explorers
and
E. E. "Doc" Smith

WARNING! ! ! !

Do not read this book straight through from beginning to end! These pages contain many different adventures you may have as a commander in the Space Patrol. From time to time as you read along, you will be asked to make a choice. Your choice may lead to success or disaster.

The adventures you take are a result of your choice. *You* are responsible because *you* choose! After you make your choice, follow the instructions to see what happens to you next.

Think carefully before you make your move. Your patrol is a difficult one. The galaxy is full of dangers. One mistake could be your last.

Good luck!

You are the commander and pilot of Space Rescue Emergency Vessel III. You are also the sole passenger aboard SREV III, unless you count Henry, the ship's computer, which would be a good idea. Henry, who is the eighth model of his type, is very sophisticated, and—according to General Computers, the company that made him—he is *absolutely reliable.*

Go on to page 2.

2

As commander, you patrol an assigned sector of the solar system. You are a member of the Space Patrol, and your job is to keep the peace and provide rescue services in space. You are there to help. You are a twenty-third century policeman, proud to wear the bright crimson and gold of the Patrol.

One of your major duties as commander in the Patrol is to be on the lookout for the pirates that constantly raid the traffic between Venus, Earth, Mars, and their satellites, and the satellites of those planets not hospitable to human life. You also provide emergency repair and medical services for ships and passengers troubled by breakdowns, meteorites, radiation storms, and the other routine hazards of space.

You spend six months in space, then go planetside for six months of rest and recreation. The tour of duty you are on now will be over in a few weeks. Patrol regulations say you must not go into space during your vacation—not even to a planet's moon. Your superiors want to make sure you don't even *think* of space during your rest.

Turn to page 4.

"Henry, we're going to Charon. There's no telling where the base in the asteroids is; it could be anywhere."

"Roger, Commander. I've got our course right here."

"OK, let's get going!" you say as you take the controls. Once you're on your way, you have some time to think and plan. No matter how many schemes you and Henry come up with, though, only two make sense.

If you decide to disguise the ship and pretend you're one of the revolutionists delivering the load of Swamp Fever Virus, turn to page 95.

If you decide to disguise your ship pretending you are in distress, and hope they offer aid so you can find out something that way, turn to page 83.

4

You have been thinking a lot about a vacation on Venus this time; it's one of the universe's best-known pleasure spots. But something in the back of your mind is nagging you to go to Earth, since you have never been there. You are also thinking about returning home to Shepard, Saturn's first artificial satellite.

Suddenly Henry interrupts your pleasant thoughts of vacation. "Commander, meteorite debris dead ahead. Shall I handle evasive maneuvers, or do you want the controls?"

Normally Henry would handle this routine matter, but things have been dull lately, and Henry feels you need some action.

If you decide to take the controls, turn to page 6.

If you let Henry do it so you can continue dreaming about vacation, turn to page 45.

"I'll take over, Henry."

You put your hands on the controls and start to thread your way between the meteorites. The radio crackles: "SREV II or SREV III. Emergency! Repeat, emergency! Closest vessel please respond immediately to Outer Rings of Saturn. Over."

SREV II is closer, you think, but not by much. Either of you can handle the call. Maybe you should take it; some action might feel good. On the other hand, why stick your neck out only a few weeks before your tour of duty ends? Besides, you are in the midst of meteorites.

If you decide to take the call, turn to page 8.

*If you decide to let SREV II handle it,
turn to page 13.*

When you get back to your ship, you find that Henry has been so worried about you that he has radioed HQ for help. You call your chief right away. He is not happy to hear from you.

"So you've been messing with that door?"

"Yes, sir, and I've opened it."

"Somehow I knew you would. You'd better get on over here and tell me about it."

You blast off for Mars. Halfway there you find yourself in the middle of a military escort. When you land, you are taken directly to jail. Nobody talks to you or tells you anything.

Your chief visits you one day, though. He looks sad. He shakes his head and says, "Sorry, kid. I did my best."

You have plenty of time in jail to think about everything you saw in the Xu'ka museum. In fact, you have the rest of your life.

The End

"Henry, tell HQ we'll take the call."

"Roger, Commander." Henry transmits your acceptance message and plots your course.

"HQ says the ship is under pirate attack, Commander. They hope to radio more information to us before we arrive."

"I hope so, too, Henry. Ready hyperdrive. Prepare to use emergency power and energize battle stations."

"Roger."

The meteorite storm is over now. You sit in your command couch. While Henry makes preparations, you empty your mind, meditating.

Henry's precise electronic voice interrupts. "All set, Commander."

"OK, Henry." You key the console switch for hyperdrive. Henry could do this. In fact, Henry can maneuver the ship himself in an emergency, but the paperwork you must send to HQ in that case is tremendous.

"Henry, I'm going to the ready room to put on my armor. Keep me posted."

"Roger, Commander." Henry sounds extremely calm. He's been programmed to sound calmer and calmer as stress builds—an effect his manufacturers are proud of. But whenever Henry gets exceedingly calm, you wonder what's the matter.

Go on to the next page.

Henry's voice comes over your suit headset as you walk back toward the bridge.

"Commander, four minutes and twenty-seven seconds to destination."

"Roger, Henry."

"A signal has just come in from HQ that the ship in distress is under attack by a single pirate vessel. Their defensive screens are holding, but the attackers are slowly increasing weapon power. Apparently they want to take hostages."

"Hmm. Thanks, Henry."

You settle in your couch and consider strategy. You decide you have only two choices.

If you try a sneak attack, turn to page 21.

If you go in blasting, turn to page 14.

You've decided to do the hull inspection. You climb into your space suit and put on your helmet.

"Henry, can you hear me?"

"Yes, Commander, your comm unit is working fine. *This* time."

"OK, cycle me out." Your helmet communicator is always giving you trouble. No matter how many times you take it apart, it has the inconvenient habit of not working at the worst possible times.

Outside, your special shoes hold you to the hull as you walk around in slow motion. Eveything on the ship appears OK. Then you notice one of your antennas looks odd. The easiest repair is to replace the whole antenna. You get a new one from the spare locker in the ship and go back out. While you're in the middle of fastening the antenna into place, Henry calls you.

"Commander, a radiation storm is approaching fast. You have exactly five minutes, thirty seconds to get inside."

"Roger, Henry. I'm almost done here. Do I have time to finish?'

"I wouldn't recommend it, but it's up to you. You'll have to finish in under two minutes."

If you hurry inside to escape the dangerous solar radiation, turn to page 38.

If you decide to finish with the antenna first, turn to page 30.

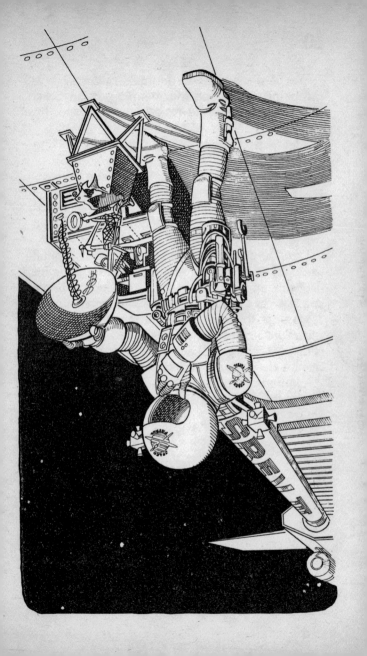

You fly toward the energy "drain." Henry keeps his sensors on the spot. As you approach the orbit of Mars, he reports that the spot has disappeared.

"Strange, Henry."

"I think so, too, Commander."

"Let's fly there anyway and see what we find."

"Roger, Commander."

When you get there you find nothing at all. You fly out a search pattern with a radius of five light-minutes, but you see nothing.

You fly through the spot itself several times— and still discover nothing. You decide to leave, but something makes you fly through the spot once more. As you do, the "drain" appears again. This time though, you are inside it. When you eventually come out the other end, you discover that you have gone back in time. You are trapped in the early twenty-first century.

You'll have a hard time convincing the primitive natives of Earth—the only planet with a human population—that you are not an alien being.

The End

"Henry, tell HQ that SREV II is closer than we are. They should take the call."

"Very good, Commander, but don't you think . . ."

"Henry!"

"Yes, Commander."

Your hands feel good on the controls as you pilot through the meteorites. The debris thins out; then it's gone entirely. Henry is getting a little pushy, you think. Maybe he needs a brain overhaul at the end of your tour. That reminds you:

"Henry, aren't we due for a visual hull check about now?"

"Yes. I was going to remind you in about an hour."

One hour. That's plenty of time to view the new holo film, *Star Wars—Episode 42,* you've been wanting to see. On the other hand, you might just as well get the hull check over with. Besides, after the meteorite storm would be a good time to check for damage.

If you decide to watch the new holo film, turn to page 28.

If you decide to do the hull inspection now, turn to page 10.

"Henry, we're going in blasting. How soon to contact?"

"Contact in one minute, fourteen seconds, Commander."

"Roger. Are all weapons at full power?"

"Yes, Commander. And our reserve capacity is at maximum."

"Good. Time now to contact?"

"Fifty-four seconds, Commander."

Just then there is an explosion at the aft end of your ship. Red lights on your console come on, and warning buzzers start screaming.

"Henry! What happened?"

"We've been hit, Commander," Henry says, very calmly, in the almost bored tone that means there's been bad damage.

"Where, Henry? Where?"

"In the propulsion unit, Commander. Our radio is out as well."

"Oh, great!" you groan. "There wasn't just one pirate ship after all. A second ship must have been waiting for us to go by, then—pow!—right in our tail. Any suggestions, Henry?"

Turn to page 16.

When you get close enough to the asteroid, you give it a visual scan.

"Looks OK, Henry. Let's set her down there, in that depression. We'll have plenty of protection from the storm."

With Henry's help you soon land safely, the asteroid between you and the storm. A phrase from your childhood runs through your mind: "Snug as a bug in a rug."

"Henry, what's a 'rug'?"

"A rug, Commander, is a term for a woven fabric that is used to cover a floor."

"What's a 'bug'?"

" 'Bug' is a slang term for a number of things. One: a glitch in a computer program. Two: a virus causing . . ."

"Cancel, Henry, cancel." You've gotten Henry into his dictionary mode. He could go on like that for hours. Besides, you're not interested anymore: you're hungry.

"Henry, dial me up some proto-soy cookies and milk. Then I'm going to take a nap. Wake me when the storm is over."

"Yes, Commander," Henry says as you head off to the galley.

Turn to page 20.

"Two, Commander. One: Since we can't change our course, we'll continue until we're spotted by HQ and they send a rescue ship to our aid. Or two: You could leave in a life-pod and head toward the ship in distress while I continue alone. My sensors indicate the pirates have left. Perhaps you can aid the passengers, if they are still there, and use their radio, if it works. If it doesn't, I can tell HQ where you are when they get to me."

If you decide to try Henry's plan with the life-pod, turn to page 60.

If you decide Henry's plan is too risky and you'd rather wait for help, turn to page 114.

You've just decided to call the repair ship when you have an idea.

"Henry, I'm having trouble with one of these sensors. We're going to need a repair ship. Please radio for one."

"Roger, Commander. I told you I was badly damaged."

You know Henry wasn't, but you let him think so; it might do him some good.

When the repair ship arrives, you tell Henry you want to gab with the crew on their ship for awhile. You lay the problem out to Fred and Linda, the technicians, who are sympathetic.

"Yeah, we understand. Those Model VIIIs can be touchy. We'll board your ship and run Henry through a series of checks, pretending just to check out those replaced sensors," says Linda.

"Sounds OK to me," you say. Off you all go.

Fred and Linda's checks show what looks like some serious trouble. They don't know what the cause is—nor what exactly could happen—but they tell you to go to a repair facility for further work.

Turn to page 113.

When you get near the ship that's retrofiring, you learn that Henry was right: it is a UR Model R8 Super, not a pirate ship. The passengers are surprised to see a Patrol vessel since nothing is the matter.

"Sorry we disturbed you," you say. "It's just a routine check."

You feel a little embarrassed when you tell Henry to compute a new course.

"Guess I should apologize for not believing you."

"That's all right, Commander. All humans make mistakes."

You cruise around Pluto and Neptune for hours, but nothing happens.

"Henry, do you find this Patrol stuff boring, too?" you finally ask.

"Please define, Commander."

"Boring. You know: nothing to do, sit around all day, wait for something to happen. B-O-R-I-N-G."

"I'm not sure I understand you completely. In any event, there's plenty to do: write reports, monitor radio transmissions, follow maintenance schedules, study . . ."

"Enough, Henry. That's exactly what I'm talking about. It's all . . . oh, forget it! I'm going to fix myself a sandwich." You get up from your command couch and, mouth watering, head to the galley, thinking about one of your favorite things in the universe—a dagwood sandwich.

Go on to the next page.

The sandwich is at least ten centimeters thick, and it hits the spot. Unfortunately, it also makes you sleepy, and you nod out in your chair.

You wake what feels like hours later. How long have you been asleep?

"Henry, I must have fallen asleep. What time is it?"

There is no answer.

Turn to page 42.

Henry wakes you about four hours later.

"The storm died down to safe levels fifty-four minutes ago, but my monitors indicated you were deep in REM sleep then, so I let you continue."

"Thanks, Henry. Open the viewports. Let's take a look at this place." The asteroid looks normal, just a large chunk of gray rock. Then you notice a faint glow in a crack.

"Henry, what's that glow?"

"Probably just some phosphorescence from the radiation storm."

But you're not sure.

If you decide to investigate the glow, turn to page 34.

If you decide Henry is right, and lift off, turn to page 33.

"Henry, we're going to sneak up on them. Show me on the display the least likely direction they could expect us to come from."

Henry lights up the display, then says worriedly, "But, Commander, my calculations show only a ten-percent chance of success if we arrive from that direction."

"Ah, yes, Henry, but I have a trick up my sleeve. Work up a course to bring us around to this sector." You punch in numbers on the console. "Let's go get 'em."

You pilot the ship to a hiding spot and tell Henry to wait for more directions.

Now comes the dangerous part. You slip out the air lock, making sure the two mirrors you have put into a pocket on the outside of your space armor are safe. You shove out into space and drift toward the pirates.

Before you can put your plan into action, though, a second pirate ship arrives and comes to rest next to the first one.

Turn to page 66.

Just as you realize this, the image starts changing again until once more you are looking at your own solar system.

As you step back from the wall, the black rectangle fades until the wall is featureless again. You step over to the right about three meters. Another black rectangle appears, and as you get closer you see a swirl of different colors—accompanied by scents—moving within it. The display lasts several minutes—but you can make nothing of it.

You walk around the perimeter of the room, studying all the displays. Some you understand; some you do not.

When you have seen them all, you know that the chamber was built by people called the Xu'ka of the planet Aa. They are a peaceful people and have learned much about both the physical universe and the mental one. You have learned some of their knowledge from the displays.

Turn to page 117.

You step into the corridor. It starts to glow blue-green instead of red. One side of the corridor is curved; the other side is flat. On the flat side, a black rectangle appears with a short explanation explaining that this corridor contains history lessons about both the Xu'ka and humankind.

You decide you don't like history lessons and try to get out the end of the corridor, but you bump into a transparent barrier. You can't leave. You shrug your shoulders. Maybe history won't be so bad.

In fact, the history lesson turns out to be fascinating. As you learn about the thousands of years of peaceful development of the Xu'ka, you can't help but compare it to the violent history of the human race.

You're so absorbed in the lesson that you don't notice that you are at the end of the corridor until you bump into it. Set into the wall at the end is a door. The end of the corridor is glowing blue-green, but the door is still glowing red.

You wonder what is behind it.

If you decide to try to open the door, turn to page 69.

If you decide to see if the invisible barrier is gone from the other end, turn to page 78.

One hour later, you finish replacing the last of the sensors. As you screw down the protective plate, you wonder about Henry. He said he thought his circuitry had been damaged, but you can find nothing wrong. He seems a little strange, but maybe you're just imagining it.

You could call a repair ship, but if they find nothing wrong, you'll look foolish. Besides, it might worry Henry, and the paperwork will take *days* to complete. Maybe you should keep an eye on Henry—it might be nothing after all.

If you decide to call a repair ship, turn to page 17.

If you decide just to keep an eye out for possible trouble, turn to page 29.

"Well, Henry, I guess that one worked out all right."

"Yes, Commander. I'm happy to see that my projection was proved wrong. Tell me, though, what were you going to do with the mirrors?"

"Ah, Henry. Everybody needs a secret now and then. Let's decide where to go now. Do you have any objection to heading out toward Pluto?"

"None, Commander."

"Good, then let's go. Plot us a course, Henry."

Turn to page 36.

You step out into the main chamber and glance around. You notice that the pedestal with the lever on it is gone. A careful look around shows it's nowhere to be seen, but there is a niche in the wall that wasn't there before.

You walk toward the niche. It begins to change colors—slowly at first, then faster and faster until the colors blur into a luminous white. A chair is in the niche. You are drawn towards it, unable to resist it. You struggle at first, but it is no use; your feet don't belong to you. Finally, you relax and sit in the chair.

Everything around you disappears; a peace settles over you, and you float in black space that you somehow know contains everything.

You realize that you're receiving one more lesson—a psychology lesson, the most important one.

When your lesson is over, you know it ALL!

You realize you have two choices now. You must choose to go to the planet Aa to thank the Xu'ka or to Earth to tell them what you've learned.

If you decide to go to Earth, turn to page 74.

If you decide to go to Aa, turn to page 53.

That hull inspection can wait until you've watched the new holo program.

"Henry, run that new holo we just got, will you?" You settle down in your relaxer chair in the lounge.

The lights dim, and soon you're deep in the film. The actors are small three-dimensional images, so real you feel you could touch them. Just as the movie is getting exciting, you hear Henry whispering to you.

"Commander, Commander."

You sigh loudly.

"What is it, Henry?"

"There's a radiation storm approaching."

"Bad, Henry?"

"My sensors can just detect the fringes, but it looks as though it could be."

Now what do you do? Ride it out and continue watching your program, or hide from it somewhere?

"Henry, is any protection nearby?"

"A small asteroid, Commander."

You'd really like to finish watching the film.

If you decide to stay where you are and weather the storm, turn to page 39.

If you decide to pilot to the asteroid, turn to page 15.

You decide just to keep an eye on Henry. After you are done with the repairs and have run Henry through a series of checks to make sure all the new sensors work, you decide you were probably crazy. Henry seems perfectly OK. You're sure you'll have no problem making it to the end of your tour.

"Well, Henry, everything looks fine. Your new sensors are working perfectly."

"Thanks, Commander," Henry says with a sparkle in his voice. "Which way shall we head?"

"Good question, Henry," you reply cheerfully.

If you decide to head for the inner planets, turn to page 54.

If you decide to head on out to Pluto's orbit, turn to page 36.

You hurry to finish replacing the antenna. Getting caught in a radiation storm is no picnic; you could be killed instantly or worse, die a slow painful death. In your haste, the wrench you are using slips out of your hand and floats away from the ship. Without thinking about it, you turn on your jets and fly after it.

"Commander, have you just left the hull?" Henry asks over the comm unit.

"Yes, I'm after a loose wrench."

"May I remind you that you have exactly two minutes, fifteen seconds until the storm hits. At your present speed and direction, it will take one minute and forty-five seconds for you to maneuver back to the hull. That means . . ."

"I know, Henry, I know. I can subtract, too. Please be quiet. I need to concentrate."

You leave the wrench and head for the hatch. This is critical. You are only in your regular space suit, not your armor. Your armor has protection against just about anything, but it's hard to move in. If you are caught in the storm in your regular suit, you could be boiled like an egg.

Turn to page 32.

"Try and get them on the comm, Henry. Tell them we'll be there as fast as we can, and boost us out of here."

"Roger, Commander."

As you get closer to the vessel, the radio reception improves. You find out that they were holed by a micrometeorite. It damaged some wiring on their drive unit, and they have no repair kit. In fact, they don't even have space suits they could have used in case the damage had been worse.

Once you get to work you find that the repair isn't hard. When you're finished you give the passengers of the disabled ship a good talking-to. You're sure they won't go anywhere now without a complete repair kit and their space suits.

"OK, Henry. That's all set. Let's get out of here."

"Which way, Commander?"

"Good question."

You're near the asteroid belt. Should you go toward the sun or toward the outer planets?

If you decide to head in toward the sun, turn to page 54.

If you decide to head toward the outer planets, turn to page 36.

You try not to panic in your effort to get back to the ship. You're closing as fast as you can. Suddenly you get an idea.

"Henry, when I'm back at the hatch I'll give you the word, and I want you to rotate the hull so that it shields me from the storm. That will give me just the time I need. OK?"

"Yes, Commander."

You get closer and closer to the hatch.

"Closing, Henry."

You touch; then you're secure to the hull.

"Barbecue, Henry."

"I beg your pardon, Commander. What do you mean?"

"Rotate! Rotate!"

You are a scholar of old space lingo. In your haste you used some slang from the earliest space days. Because of Henry's hesitation, you made it to the hatch but were not completely protected when the first of the storm hit. You were lucky, though; you were only blinded.

The End

"I agree, Henry. That glow is probably nothing. Let's get out of here. Prepare us for lift-off."

"Yes, Commander," Henry says. "Blast off in fifteen seconds."

You sink into your seat. "I wonder which way to go once we're off this chunk of rock," you think as your hands go to their positions on the control panel.

If you decide to head to the outer planets, turn to page 36.

If you decide to head in toward the sun, turn to page 54.

"Henry, I'm going to check out that glow," you say as you head for the air lock.

Once suited and out of the air lock, you use your jets to fly over to the glow. Since the asteroid has almost no gravity, walking would be difficult.

As you gain altitude and get closer to the glow, you can clearly see it grow larger.

It's a door!

You can't tell just how big it is, but it looks fairly big, and there appears to be a portal around it—with writing on it.

"Henry, you're not going to believe this!"

"I believe anything, Commander."

"It's a door, Henry. And it's glowing."

"You're right. I don't believe it. Are you sure?"

"You bet. My suit monitors show no dangerous

radiation, either. I'm going to take a closer look."

"Commander, Regulation 49-26-35 requires us to report newly discovered alien artifacts immediately upon discovery. Shall I radio HQ now?"

If you decide to take a look first so you'll have more to report, turn to page 56.

If you decide to follow regulations and report the door before taking a closer look, turn to page 57.

You've decided to head toward the outer planets. The distances here are greater, so less is happening than around the inner planets, which are closer together.

All the space out here, however, gives pirates and other criminals plenty of room to do their evil deeds and then escape. In fact, you received a briefing two days ago about a band of pirates who, strangely enough, were preying on the scientific traffic between Neptune and Pluto.

As you pass Jupiter, Henry reports that he has detected ship retrofire in the distance.

"My spectrographic analysis is that it is the firing of a United Rocket Model R8 Super."

"Could it be a ship in distress, Henry?"

"There is a 98.5% probability that it is not. It hardly seems worth investigating. The pirate activity we were warned about is not in this area, but eighty light-minutes away."

If you decide to investigate the retrofire anyway, turn to page 18.

If you decide Henry's probably right and the retrofire isn't worth investigating, turn to page 80.

"OK, Henry, I'm coming in. I'll finish up later."

The storm hits after you are safely inside and have taken off your suit.

"It's a bad storm, Commander. I'm glad you're inside." Henry sounds relieved.

"Me, too, Henry," you say as you slide into the pilot's couch. "I'd rather *eat* a hard-boiled egg than *be* one."

"Distress signal coming in, Commander."

". . . ayday. Mayday . . . is FBR34 . . . holed by . . . ayday."

"Henry, see if you can get a fix on that signal. The storm is interfering with radio reception."

"Commander, I've pinpointed the signal," Henry says a few minutes later. "I've also enhanced the signal. They're a private vessel, hit by a micrometeorite. They're located here." Henry lights up the location on your nav screen.

Turn to page 31.

"Henry, I want to watch the rest of this holo. We'll stay here. Please don't disturb me unless it's absolutely necessary."

"Yes, Commander," Henry says sulkily.

The holo ends about forty minutes later.

"Well, Henry, I guess it's time to do that hull inspection." Then you remember. "Oh, what happened with the radiation storm?"

"It's letting up now, Commander. The peak passed about twenty-four minutes ago."

"Is it safe to do the hull inspection?"

"I couldn't tell you, Commander," Henry says haughtily. "Some of my sensors were damaged. Possibly some circuitry was knocked out, too." Henry sounds as though he's blaming you.

"Oh, Henry, you're probably OK," you say, but you go through a systems check anyway.

"Henry, it looks as if there's just some damage to those sensors of yours."

"Yes, Commander." Now Henry sounds like a little kid who's skinned his knee.

"I'm sure the rad storm has died down enough to do that hull inspection and replace those sensors."

Turn to page 24.

"I'm not sure what to do now, Henry. Any thoughts?"

"I suppose, Commander, that we can only keep on trying the radio."

"I just thought of another possibility, Henry. I could put on a space suit and go down there myself."

If you decide to keep trying the call for help, turn to page 88.

If you decide to go down to the surface, turn to page 108.

You decide to check some of the service panels on the outside of the ship and head to the air lock to put on your space suit. Once outside, you head over to a likely panel and remove the covering. A careful look shows no sign of any damage. The same thing happens with the next three panels, but the fourth one comes off to reveal a burned mess.

Now what could have done that? There's no telling. You slip inside to get some spare parts and head back out.

You fix some of the damage and try to reach Henry on your suit radio—but still get nothing. The rest of the service panels look fine. You decide to give up and call HQ when it happens!

Turn to page 85.

"Henry!" you call again. More silence.

You hurry up to the bridge. Maybe there's just something wrong with the speaker in the lounge, but Henry doesn't answer your shouts in the corridor or on the bridge.

Quickly you run through a series of tests on the ship's computer. Everything seems normal—all the ship's systems appear to be operating—except for Henry's program. Somehow Henry isn't there at all, which is very strange. Where can a computer or computer program go? It can't pick itself up and walk away!

You decide to try the radio to see if it works. "This is SREV III. This is a test. Can anyone hear my signal? Repeat. This is SREV . . ."

"This is Patrol Base Pluto, SREV III. We read you loud and clear. Is anything the matter?"

If you decide to tell them Henry is missing, turn to page 82.

If you decide not to tell—not yet anyway—and to investigate some more yourself, turn to page 75.

"Well, the probabilities are pretty even, Henry, but the first plan has a slightly greater chance of success, so we'll go with it. Besides, my trigger finger is itchy."

"Roger, Commander. Ready whenever you are. Defensive screens are deployed. All weapons are energized."

"Keep your eye on the large ship, Henry."

"Just a second. I'm intercepting another radio message, Commander."

"Let's hear it, Henry."

"So you refuse my demands. You leave me no choice then, madam. Engineering, prepare to blow them out of the sky!"

"Fire, Henry!"

Turn to page 118.

44

You can hear the fear in Dr. Grotch's voice. You're not too happy yourself. Venusian Swamp Fever is deadly—and it causes a very painful death. There is no known cure, and since it's highly infectious, it can wipe out millions of people in twenty-four hours. It came from somewhere in the swamps of Venus, a by-product of the terra-forming, and killed thousands of people working there before it was brought under control. How did somebody get a dose of it now? you wonder. Well, it's no matter. You know what you have to do.

"Dr. Grotch, please let me speak to your pilot."

"Pilot Joy Arnveldt here."

"Pilot Arnveldt, this is the commander of Space Rescue Emergency Vessel III. Under the authority of the Space Patrol, I hereby direct you to change course immediately to the flight path my computer will give you in a moment. I must warn you that if you do not change course within five seconds I am empowered to vaporize your ship immediately. In addition, I have your ship under total surveillance. Anything leaving your ship will be destroyed. Do you understand?"

"Yes, Commander."

"Henry, send them a course to take them into the sun."

Turn to page 50.

"You handle the controls, Henry."

Unfortunately, hidden among the meteorites is an unexploded bomb left over from the Second Solar System War fifty Earth years ago. Henry's course takes you too close, much too close, and you, Henry, and the ship are instantly vaporized.

The End

"Henry, I'm afraid we don't have time for spying. Something tells me we're running against the clock here."

"I'll get HQ, then."

Henry puts the call through, and soon the mine is surrounded by Patrol ships. You tell the chief of the search operation that you believe this place might be a cover for a secret operation involving deadly diseases. He scoffs at your idea but says, "I'll tell you what. You come, too, and look around for yourself."

But you find nothing that supports your theory. The prospectors working the asteroid had simply discovered a wealth of diamonds and decided to keep their find a secret.

Nothing here links with the scheme to take over the solar system. You must keep looking.

If you decide to check out the resort facility, turn to page 71.

If you decide to take a look at the energy "drain," turn to page 12.

If you decide to abandon the asteroid belt for now and go to Charon, turn to page 3.

"Commander, I must confess," says the victim. "I didn't know what was happening. I've got to tell you all this before I die. I was told to pick up this capsule and bring it back—"

"What capsule? From whom? Bring it back where?" You need facts.

"Please, Commander, I don't have much time. Let me get this out my own way. The capsule was in a locker in the Venus spaceport. I never saw anybody. I was bringing it back to Charon—you know, Pluto's moon. We have a base there."

"We?" You can't help interrupting.

"We're a group of revolutionists. We want to get rid of our peaceful civilization. We feel that the old philosophy of war brought out the best in humanity. But honest, I didn't know it was Swamp Fever I was picking up." He sobs loudly. "That stuff is awful!" He catches his sobs, then continues. "My group—we don't have a name, it's easier to stay hidden that way—my group is collecting deadly viruses from all over, but mostly from the disease research centers on Pluto and Uranus, to use to spread dissention and disorder among the populated planets . . ."

"But how?" you break in.

"Right now we're working on an operating base in the asteroid belt. We'll work our plan from there. It's . . ."

It's too late. He never finishes. The explosion destroys both him and the communicator.

Go on to the next page.

You radio HQ and tell them everything that has happened, except what the victim told you before he blew up. You're afraid they won't believe you; it sounds too farfetched.

HQ sends more Patrol ships to escort the ferry on its trip to the sun. So far, no more cases have shown up, and it's likely it won't have to be destroyed. You're glad for that.

Now you feel you should investigate what the victim told you, but you're not sure what to do.

If you decide to go to Charon and check out the base there, turn to page 3.

If you decide to try to find the new base in the asteroid belt, turn to page 52.

The *Merry Ferry* changes course and you fly in close escort. It has two hours before it will run into the sun and be vaporized.

Venusian Swamp Fever is a terrible disease. Five minutes after contact with the disease, the victim's temperature soars. After fifteen minutes his limbs fall off. After twenty-five minutes his body starts to expand until he is as round as a ball. Then he blows up, releasing trillions of viruses to infect other people.

You get Dr. Grotch on the radio again and learn that the person with the disease hasn't blown up yet. You're not sure how this person got the disease, but if you can get him into a life-pod before he blows up, there is a chance that you may not have to destroy the ferry and all its passengers.

The ferry does as you direct, and the victim is safely ejected about five minutes before he starts to expand. At this point in the disease, the fever subsides and the victim becomes lucid—totally aware of what is happening right up to the second he explodes.

The victim aboard the life-pod wants to talk to you on the radio. It must be something very important.

Turn to page 48.

You decide it's got to be the asteroid belt. There's no telling how far along the criminals are in their plans, and you *must* stop them.

The only problem is that the asteroid belt is immense. The criminals could be anywhere. In addition, the mining and manufacturing operations that go on there could provide a cover for just about anything.

"Henry," you say, thinking fast, "we need lots of data, sorted quickly."

"Roger, Commander."

With Henry to help, you sort through all the data you can find about the asteroid belts. Then you scan the belt yourself. You end up with three interesting discoveries.

One: A resort is being built on one large asteroid. Your data shows that more material is being shipped there than is needed.

Two: In one area of the belt, an unusually high number of people have disappeared.

Three: Another spot appears to be an energy "drain." That is, large amounts of energy seem to be "disappearing" in the spot.

If you decide to check out the resort construction site, turn to page 71.

If you decide to go instead to the area where the people are disappearing, turn to page 104.

If you decide to see what the energy "drain" is, turn to page 12.

You go back to your ship. Henry is dismayed at how long you have been gone, but with your new knowledge it is easy to calm and reassure him. You also use your new knowledge to make a few modifications on your ship.

When you are done, you press a green button on your control panel that wasn't there before. You are instantly transported to an orbit around the planet Aa.

The Xu'ka are glad to see you. As for you, you feel you've come home.

The End

You have decided to head for the inner planets. This area is the most densely populated of the solar system. You pass Earth and are coming up on Venus. You are about to tell Henry you've decided to do an orbit around the sun and head back out when a distress call comes in from the Earth-Venus shuttle.

"Any Patrol vessel. Repeat, any Patrol vessel. This is Dr. Armand Grotch, physician aboard the shuttle *Merry Ferry*. We have a medical emergency. Repeat, medical emergency!" The signal comes in loud and strong. Henry reports they're almost next door.

"Dr. Grotch, this is the commander of SREV III. What seems to be the trouble? Over."

"Commander, we have a case of—" Dr. Grotch stops. You can hear an argument in the background.

"We've got to report it."

"But we're not certain."

"I am. Do you know what will happen to the Earth if we touch down with this disease aboard?" Then you hear Dr. Grotch talking to you again.

"Commander, we have a case of Venusian Swamp Fever aboard. Over."

Turn to page 44.

As you fly closer, you keep studying the door. You're still unable to judge its size, but it must be huge—it keeps getting bigger and bigger.

Finally you can clearly see the markings on the portal. It's alien writing! It is not like any you have ever seen.

Your suit computer has calculated a perfect course and landing. You come in three meters away and land on your feet. You need to bend your knees only slightly to cushion the touchdown as you land facing the door.

At this distance you see that the glow from the door has a pattern to it. It is familiar but not something you recognize. You can now judge that the door is huge: ten meters high and four meters wide. The portal is even more massive than the door.

For a moment you are speechless; then slowly you whisper one of your favorite expressions: "Holy smokes!"

The door slides open instantly.

Turn to page 58.

You use your suit computer to stop your flight.

"OK, Henry. Patch me through to HQ."

You report your discovery to your chief. To your surprise, he materializes as a small hologram in front of you. This must be something big!

"I had a feeling you'd be the first of my crew to discover this; you've always been right on the scene when something happens.

"This site has been classified. You'll have to clear out immediately and forget you've ever seen it."

"Why, Chief?"

"Well, I shouldn't tell you this, but nobody has figured out a way to get in that door. Scientists and engineers have tried everything, and it won't budge. The higher-ups believe the door is from an alien civilization that we know nothing about, and that the aliens will give us the secret to the door when they feel we're ready—but not before.

"In the meantime, the word is that *nobody* messes with it. So flit on out of there. And that's an order."

Turn to page 62.

As you step through the doorway, the chamber inside begins to glow—a dim blue-green which slowly gets brighter until you can see the room you are in. It's a circular space about twenty meters across, with a high, vaulted ceiling. The light is now a bright white, but the walls seem to glow pale blue or green—you can't tell which.

You are looking around, craning your neck and trying to determine where the light is coming from, when a voice speaks to you in your head.

"Greeting, Human."

The voice seems loud, but it doesn't hurt. It has a hollow, echoing ring.

"We mean you no harm," the voice continues. "Pull the lever on the pedestal to learn the secrets of the universe."

"Who are you?" you say, but there is no answer.

The pedestal is in the middle of the room—was it there before? The lever is sticking out of the side at an angle. An arrow on the pedestal points down.

If you decide to pull the lever, turn to page 68.

If you decide to take a look around first, turn to page 65.

60

"Henry, your plan sounds crazy, but I've tried some of your plans that sounded crazier—and they worked. So let's go!"

You jump inside the life-pod. You barely have the hatch closed when you hear Henry start the countdown.

"Five seconds, Commander. Three, good, two, luck, one, fire!'

You are shot out into space, close to the disabled ship. There is no sign of the pirates.

Once aboard the ship you discover that nobody is aboard; the pirates must have taken all the passengers. You make your way to the bridge to check out the radio. It works! When you finish sending your report to HQ you have the odd feeling you are not alone.

Turn to page 64.

The chief winks out, and you are alone again—floating over the asteroid.

The chief certainly sounds as if he means it. But sometimes he comes on stronger than he needs to, and you do have a knack for keeping out of trouble. It wouldn't hurt just to take a closer look, would it?

If you decide to take a closer look, turn to page 115.

If you decide you'd better leave, go on to the next page.

"Henry, I'm coming back. We'd better follow orders and leave here. Prepare to take me aboard."

"Roger, Commander."

You cycle back through the lock.

"Where to now, Commander?"

"Let's see, Henry. Put up the nav display."

But instead of the nav display, Henry lights up an illustration of Alice contemplating whether to go down the rabbit hole. You recognize the picture from the famous tricentennial edition of *Alice in Wonderland.*

"Good joke, Henry, but I've already decided not to follow the rabbit through the door."

"I thought you'd like it," Henry says in a pleased tone as he shifts the screen to the nav display.

The nav display is a picture of the solar system with your position indicated. Also shown are the routes of the various passenger ships and regular freight runs between the planets, and any known positions of the other Space Rescue ships.

"Well, Henry, it looks as if we could go in any direction."

Turn to page 116.

You turn around quickly, your laser gun drawn—but all you see is a little girl in a space suit. She looks your crimson and gold over.

"You're Space Patrol?"

You nod yes.

"Oh, good. My daddy made me hide until help arrived."

"Did everyone else get taken away by the pirates?"

"Yes, and they're not pirates. Daddy said they're kidnappers trying to keep him from going to an important meeting for his company."

"I see."

"Yes, and I know which way they went. I'm a Space Scout, so I knew what to do. I sneaked up to the bridge before you came and used the plotting scope. Here's their speed and trajectory," she says proudly as she hands you a printout.

"Fantastic!" you say. You relay her information to HQ immediately. They report that SREV VIII is in a position to intercept.

As for Henry, he discovered after you left that his sensors, not the propulsion unit, had been destroyed. Once he realized what had happened, he turned around, and now he is on his way back to pick you up.

The End

You decide to look around before pulling the lever. Your suit monitors show that the room is filled with breatheable air. You take off your helmet and glance around.

The walls look featureless from where you stand. But as you take a few steps toward your left, a rectangle of wall changes from the blue or green glow and becomes black.

When you are about one meter from the wall you can see that the rectangle is not solid black. There is one glowing ball in its center. As you look more closely, you see some more dots in it, and they're moving. Of course! It's the solar system. All the planets are revolving around the sun.

Then you notice that everything is getting smaller. Soon you cannot see the planets, only the small glowing spot that is the sun. The other stars of the galaxy appear. Suddenly you feel as if you're spinning away from them, flying rapidly out of the galaxy.

The illusion is so real that you look around you in panic. The chamber is still there; you have not moved. You turn back to the display. You now see the spiral shape of the Milky Way galaxy. It continues growing smaller until a huge lens-shaped galaxy comes into view. You change direction and fly into that galaxy until you are focused on one medium-sized yellowish star with twelve planets circling it. Of course! This must be the home system of the aliens who made this place.

Turn to page 22.

Space-suited figures leave the first ship and use their suit jets to fly to the second. One figure is wrapped in a cocoon of orange light. He is a captive. You wait for them at the air lock of the second ship, laser gun in hand, concealed in the shadow of a hull protrusion.

Suddenly you are spotted!

Silent laser beams flash through the space between you and a figure grinning evilly behind its helmet. He misses! You score a direct hit!

"This is it. Drop your weapons," you command. "You are surrounded. I arrest you in the

name of the Patrol. One false move and it's all over."

You escort the captive back to his ship and tell Henry to call for reinforcements to take the prisoners to jail.

Once the prisoners are on their way to jail and their victim is safely on his way, you go back to your ship.

Turn to page 25.

You pull the lever.

Instantly you are surrounded by a swirling whiteness. You're not sure if you're there for an instant or an eternity, but you learn that you are being transported to the planet Aa by the makers of the museum you entered. They are called Xu'ka.

On their home planet you will learn all the secrets of the universe.

The End

In the middle of the door is an indentation, but otherwise nothing mars its smooth surface.

"That must be the latch," you think. "I touch my hand on that spot to open the door."

You put your helmet under your left arm and raise your right arm to the door. When your hand is inches from the spot you stop suddenly. Something about the whole setup is bothering you.

Why is the door still glowing red—the danger color—when everything else in the corridor has changed to blue-green? You look more closely at the door.

It must be an air lock! If you didn't have gloves on, you'd snap your fingers.

And that explains the transparent barrier at the other end. As soon as you touch that spot, air in the corridor will be evacuated and the door will open into space.

Whew! It's a good thing you stopped. Now you're wondering if you want to open that door after all.

If you decide to put on your helmet and activate the door, turn to page 76.

If you've changed your mind about the door and decide to leave it for later, turn to page 26.

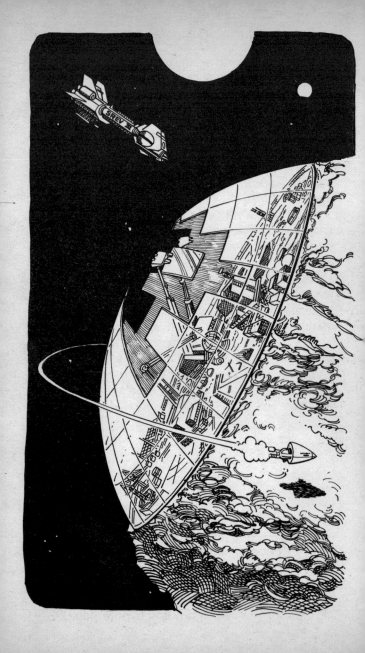

"Henry, let's go to the resort construction site. It sounds like the least likely spot, but that doesn't mean anything."

"Sounds illogical, but you're the commander."

You fly over to the construction site. One end of the asteroid has been cut flat. The rock removed is being used to construct a large dome there.

The place looks perfectly ordinary. You decide you'll find nothing just by looking around. Then Henry says, "Commander, I have a thought. A construction worker might find out firsthand something that somebody just looking around wouldn't see. It should be easy to get yourself hired as a worker. In a day or two you would know if anything fishy is going on."

You like Henry's plan, but you're also thinking of the direct approach. "Good idea, Henry. I have another possibility. I could pretend I'm bringing in a load of Venusian Swamp Virus and see what happens. I'm a good bluffer."

If you decide to try Henry's plan, put on your work clothes and turn to page 86.

If you try your idea, make up a false hollow tooth and turn to page 92.

You find yourself in a long corridor and decide to go aft to examine the power plant. To your surprise you do not discover the modern faster-than-light system that you know, but an ancient atomic reactor.

You try to examine the reactor more closely, but your suit monitors suddenly come on with a loud screeching: the pile must still be active and poorly-shielded. You leave immediately.

As you walk down the long corridor toward the cockpit, you notice a strange design on the wall. When you stop to examine it, it becomes an opening, and from within you hear a voice.

"Greeting, Human. Please enter," says the voice.

You would like to leave the ship, but discover you have lost your way.

Meekly following instructions, you sit down. No one is in the room.

"Hey!" you call. "Where are you? Is anybody here?"

"I am here," the voice responds.

"Why can't I see you?"

"Because I am incorporeal—I have no body."

"Then how do you speak?"

"It's a mystery."

"Oh," you say. It doesn't seem as if you're getting very far. You try again. "Why did you invite me in here, or is that a mystery too?"

Go on to the next page.

"No, Human, it is not a mystery." You hear a slight cough. How can somebody who doesn't have a throat cough? The voice continues, "Into some people's lives, Human, comes the chance to serve for the good of all beings.

"You have that chance. You have just enlisted in the Time Investigation Control League. At the moment this ship is traveling into the past, where, if you pay careful attention to instructions and detail—and if you are lucky—you will enter a computer control room, flip a switch, and avert a tragedy that has no business existing.

"I will tell you more, but you must rest now."

"Hey, wait a min—" you start to say. You want to know more, but you're fast asleep before you finish.

Enjoy your nap. Destiny awaits.

The End

You decide to go to Earth to tell people about the wonders of the Xu'ka museum.

The people of Earth are not happy to learn that they don't know everything. They are extremely upset with you.

You are taken to trial for disobeying orders and for tampering with a classified site. The judge orders a brain-wipe for you, and you are sent to the moon to be a farmer.

You spend the rest of your life hoeing beans, thinking you have forgotten something or other.

The End

If you don't like this ending, turn to page 87.

"No, Pluto Base, there's nothing the matter," you say. "I, uh, thought there might have been some refragilation with the radio's—uh—frimication circuitry, but I guess there's no problem. Thanks. SREV III over and out."

Well, that takes care of that. Now the problem is to find out what happened to Henry and fix him. You lean back in your command couch in your favorite thinking posture—hands clasped behind your head—and wonder what might have caused this problem. You finally come up with two possibilities.

The radiation storm may have caused some damage to the ship's and Henry's circuitry. Perhaps you should check some of the service panels on the outside of the hull.

And you remember that you were annoyed with Henry just before you went to the galley and yelled "forget it" at him. You don't know if this has done anything, but it might be worth investigating.

If you decide to check the service panels, turn to page 41.

If you decide to determine whether Henry is "upset," turn to page 91.

You put on your helmet and touch your hand to the door.

The door starts changing color, from red toward infrared, then purple, then black. The readout in your helmet indicates a sudden drop in air pressure in the corridor. The door becomes invisible. The frame around it glows yellow. You can see the gray rocks of the asteroid and stars through the doorway.

You put your hand where the door was. Nothing! You step out into a small cave in the asteroid. The floor of the cave is smooth stone. It looks as if it has been cut and polished with a laser. There are no lights in the cave, but the sun is shining in.

Then you notice the glint of sunlight on bright metal.

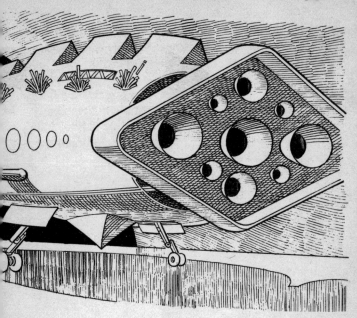

"Why, it's a space ship!" you exclaim out loud. You take a few steps closer for a better look.

The ship is of a strange design. You decide it must belong to the Xu'ka.

"Something is definitely weird about this ship," you say to yourself. "I wonder if it's safe to go aboard it, or if I should leave it alone for now."

If you decide to take a closer look at the ship, turn to page 79.

If you decide to go back inside, turn to page 90.

You decide to see if the barrier is gone from the other end of the corridor. If it isn't, you decide, then you can see about opening the door.

You start to walk briskly down the corridor, but you're stopped by the last black rectangle you looked at. It has come on again, but shows a different display. Instead of a history lesson, it is now a science lesson. You walk slowly down the corridor examining all the displays.

The first starts with a ball rolling down an inclined plane. From there it proceeds to touch on every concept of Newtonian physics. Each succeeding display expands on the knowledge of the last until—without your knowing quite what has happened—you have learned the answers to questions your professors of physics, chemistry, and mathematics were unable to answer themselves.

Turn to page 81.

You walk up to the ship. You see no markings on the hull and no way to enter the ship, but you do find a very strange-looking propulsion section—at least, that's what you guess it is.

You move closer to the ship and walk around more slowly this time. You still find no sign of an entry. Just when you decide it's no use and you start to leave, an opening appears in the side of the hull, and a stairway descends to the ground.

You climb up and step in.

Turn to page 72.

"Stay on our course, Henry," you say. "You're probably right about that just being retrofire. But keep an ear out for any strange radio transmissions."

"Yes, Commander," Henry says.

Soon you leave Neptune far behind. Pluto, however, is a long way off when Henry interrupts you while you are working at your desk, trying to make sense of some new regulations.

"Excuse me, Commander, I've intercepted a radio call from somewhere near Saturn. The signal is weak. It sounds like a distress call. Shall I play it for you?"

"Yes, but let's head in that direction first. If it is a distress call, we'd better get there as fast as we can!"

On your way to Saturn, Henry plays the message for you. It says simply: "Help! Help! Leave me alone, you beast!" Henry says the transmission was not on one of the wavelengths normally used for distress calls or regular commercial traffic.

Turn to page 93.

When your science lesson is over, you realize with a start that you've lost track of time. You hold your helmet up to check its time display: four hours have gone by! Henry must be in a snit wondering what's happened to you. Since you have been in the chamber you have been unable to contact him on the radio—you have been assuming there was some kind of shielding blocking your signals.

"Wait a minute," you think. What was on that last display you saw? Oh, right! Clever, clever . . . perfect, undetectable, electromagnetic shielding.

Then you remember Henry again.

If you decide to go back to the ship now to reassure Henry, turn to page 7.

If you decide Henry is probably at his maximum programmed limit for worry, and you should keep looking around, turn to page 26.

"Uh, yes, Pluto Base. It's kind of hard to explain, but—well, my ship's computer is missing."

"What do you mean *missing*? Somebody *stole* it?"

"Well, no. That's not what I mean. The computer is here—I mean, the hardware is here, but *Henry* isn't."

"Henry isn't? This is highly irregular, Commander. You'd better fly to the General Repair Facility at Moon Base immediately. Over and out."

At the repair facility you're questioned thoroughly, but nobody tells you what's going on. Finally you are called into your chief's office. You're prepared for the worst, but the chief is smiling.

"Well, we found Henry. It wasn't easy, though. It seems that you told Henry to 'forget it.' But Henry can't forget anything that's related directly to ship function. What he *could* forget was who he is. Henry took your phrase as an order. He 'forgot' himself—and virtually disappeared."

"But Henry's OK now?" you ask.

"Yes, he's fine now. And thanks to you we're ordering a recall on all ships of this make so that this type of incident won't happen again—we hope.

"Anyway," the chief continues, "you're dismissed now. Go and say hello to Henry, and then your tour of duty is ended. You may start your vacation a little early. Thanks—and have fun."

You plan to.

The End

"Henry, we're in trouble."

"We are? What's wrong?" Henry sounds surprised.

"No, not that. I mean we're going to pretend we're in trouble. We're going to be—let's see—yes, a trader coming from . . . from Tau Ceti, and we've lost our FTL drive somewhere near the solar system. We've had to complete the journey on our reaction jets, but they've broken down, too. And . . . oh yeah, our radio has conked out; we only have this low-power rig with barely enough juice to make it down to the planet surface. How's that sound?"

"Weird, but OK."

"Then let's get going."

You use the false plating and other equipment aboard to disguise your ship. Henry calculates a course and you appear above Charon, coming from just the proper direction and at the proper speed as though your story were true.

You get on the radio and send a mayday, a low-power, carefully worded message beamed toward the moon's surface. You throw in the information that you are carrying the only known sample in this solar system of a particularly deadly disease from the Tau Ceti region. "That should wake them up," you tell Henry—but it doesn't. You get no response.

Turn to page 40.

Suddenly you're spinning through space! "There must be a malfunction in my suit jets. Oh well," you think calmly, "I'll call Henry and have him maneuver . . . uh-oh!" No Henry! Now what?

"Oh, Henry, where are you when I need you?" you whisper.

"Right here, of course," comes the familiar voice.

"Henry! Where have you been?"

"Been? I haven't been anywhere. What are you doing out there?"

"I'm not sure, Henry," you say with a laugh. "Come pick me up, though."

Henry does as you ask, and soon you are reunited with him. You never do find out exactly what happened, and you don't really care. You're just glad he's back.

The End

Henry tells you to be careful.

"Space workers can be good people, but they can also be a rough lot. Don't get into any brawls."

"OK, Henry," you reassure him. He sounds like your mother.

The woman in the personnel office tells you they're only hiring welders now. You say, "That's great, because I'm the best welder that's ever climbed into a space suit!" She gives you a funny look, but she hires you anyway.

Your supervisor turns out to be a grizzled old man with no legs. He uses his arms to pull himself around. He gives you a long lecture on job performance and tells you where you'll bunk, where the recreation module is, and what the hours are.

"Sounds OK," you say.

"You've got two hours left on your work shift. Get suited and go over there." He points to a site. "Ask for Paul. He'll put you to work."

You turn to go, but he stops you before you're out the door.

Turn to page 94.

One day you put down your hoe. You sit in a lotus position and start to meditate.

After four days, the knowledge you had before your brain-wipe starts to seep back into your brain. You discover that it had all been stored in your big toe.

You leave your body behind and join your mind with the Xu'ka.

The End

"Let's keep trying, Henry. We can always do something else later."

"Roger, Commander."

You put the mayday message on automatic and lean back in your command couch for a rest. Finally Henry breaks in:

"We got 'em! A message is coming in from Charon."

"Hello, Trader. This is a research base on Charon. We are receiving your message. A rescue ship will be launched shortly. Stand by for assistance."

You're worried. The reply sounds almost too ordinary. Maybe there really is just a research station here. Oh, well—you're committed now!

"Full alert, Henry. Let's get ready to meet our visitors."

Turn to page 107.

The instant the screens are down, the rescue ship fires a volley of laser shots at you. They'd vaporize you in an instant if your screens weren't there to block them. Instead, they bounce off harmlessly. It is a quick matter to disable the other ship with your own guns.

Once that's taken care of, you radio HQ and tell them the whole story. When help arrives, you take over the base on Charon. You find everything you suspect, including stocks of deadly diseases and evidence of their entire plan.

But you always suspect that you didn't catch everybody and that someday, somebody will be back again.

The End

Something about this ship is too weird. You step back into the corridor. The door reappears behind you, but you don't notice.

Your mind is a strange jumble of facts, visions, and impressions. You can't seem to think for all the information that is crammed in your head.

You make your way back to your own ship in a daze and command Henry to lift off immediately. You collapse in the sick bay. It takes all Henry's medical skill to keep you alive and functioning.

While you are not conscious to the universe, your mind is still working—trying to make sense of everything you have seen and been taught. When all your new knowledge is in order, you will awaken. Who knows what the result will be, but it will be *something*!

The End

The more you think about it, the less certain you are that yelling at Henry had anything to do with the problem. Still, it's worth a shot.

You lean forward toward the terminal. Rapidly your fingers hit the keys.

100 *Command: Cancel command, last, verbal*
200 *Run*

You lean back, done. But then, almost without thinking about it, you lean over and type some more.

Henry, I'm sorry I yelled at you. I apologize.

Now you feel better, but there is still no response from Henry.

This may take some time. You decide to finish that nap you started, and you head off to bed.

Hours later you awaken from a deep sleep. Somebody is singing! It's coming from the bridge!

As you race down the corridor, you recognize Henry's voice! Then you make out the words.

"Oh . . . I'm 'Enery the Eighth I am. 'Enery the Eighth I am, I am."

A big grin comes to your face, and you breathe a sigh of relief.

He's back!

The End

"Henry, I'm going to try the direct approach," you say.

"My calculations don't give much chance of success, but you're in charge."

"Right, Henry."

You put on your armor. It's bright crimson with the Patrol insignia in gold. You jet to the large sphere Henry has picked as a suspicious spot. This bluff had better work.

A careful look at the smooth sphere shows you the only entrance. You float in front of it and palm the lock open. As the door starts to open, you say:

"Open in the name of the Patrol!" The space-suited guard who is on the other side is petrified at the sight of a Patrol commander.

"Take me to the boss," you order.

"R-right away!"

You are led through a maze of corridors until you finally come to an unmarked door.

"In—in there," the guard stammers. You step into what looks like an ordinary office. A distinguished-looking older man is sitting at a desk typing into a computer terminal.

"What?" He turns and looks at you. You think he looks frightened, but he sounds normal. "Oh! Why, Commander, to what do we owe the pleasure?"

Instead of answering, you take off your helmet and put it under your arm. You stare at him. Then you laugh.

Turn to page 99.

"Henry, something sounds fishy to me. I'm putting on my armor. Prepare us for battle, and see if you can get a better fix on the location as we get closer."

"Roger, Commander."

When you return to the bridge in your space armor, Henry says he has intercepted another message. It's the same as before. And he has pinpointed the origin of the call. It is coming from Saturn's moon, Mimas.

"Good work, Henry. Calculate a course that will take us there as fast as possible. And execute non-detectable mode as we pass Tethys's orbit."

Once you are on your way, you lean back to think. For the umpteenth time you're grateful for this mode, which gives you almost perfect invisibility.

Henry breaks into your thoughts. "Commander, we are now passing Tethys. I have a picture of the situation." He flashes up a hologram of the area around Mimas.

Turn to page 101.

"Oh, and stay away from that"—he points to a large free-floating structure out in space—"and from the other end of this asteroid."

"Why?"

"Don't ask stupid questions. Just do it. Now get out!"

You leave, but you know you won't do what he says.

If you decide to check out the other end of the asteroid as soon as you're done with work, turn to page 109.

If you decide to check out the large pod in space, turn to page 105.

You decide to pretend to be the man carrying the Swamp Virus. Before you left the *Merry Ferry,* Dr. Grotch told you the name on the man's papers was George Chumpfeffer. You don't know if that was his real name, but it's all you've got. It'll have to do.

Disguising the ship is easy. You put false plating into place and fit nameplates with the United Rockets *Starfire* logotype right over the Patrol insignia. You even dump top-secret chemicals into the maneuvering jets to give a false spectrographic reading. When you're done, your ship looks exactly like a UR *Starfire.*

With the disguise ready, you stop just far enough away so that you cannot be detected.

"I've completed my scans, Commander," Henry says presently.

"Good work, Henry. What do you have?"

"A little infrared radiation coming from this spot here." He lights up a point on the display of Charon. "There must be a dome hidden there that is leaking heat. My noise scan also shows a radio there, tuned to receive this frequency." Henry lights up the information on the display.

"Good work, Henry! Let's go get 'em."

"Roger, Commander, and good luck."

"Thanks, Henry."

Carefully you fly to a spot over the dome. The radio is set at the proper frequency.

"Hello, Base. This is Chumpfeffer," you say, imitating him as best as you can. "I've got the delivery."

Go on to the next page.

The response is immediate. "Leave your ship where it is. Bring the shipment in yourself."

You don't know whether this is normal procedure, but you have no choice. You were lucky to get this far; you have to go all the way.

You hustle into your space suit. You wish you could use your armor, but it is too distinctive; you'd give yourself away immediately.

Henry wishes you luck again as you cycle out of the air lock and cast off with a wave.

Unfortunately for you, a laser cannon vaporizes you instantly as you are halfway to Charon.

Henry is able to keep the ship from destruction with the defensive screens. He calls in reinforcements from the Patrol. The inhabitants of the dome are all captured.

But nobody is ever sure whether they got all the plotters.

The End

"Hold tight on the screens, Henry," you say. "We'll wait and see what develops. But be ready to turn them on instantly."

"Roger, Commander."

Unfortunately, though, Henry is not quick enough with the screens. You are engulfed in a deadly ball of laser fire.

The End

"Scared you, didn't I? It's a nice disguise. It looks just like real Patrol armor."

"*What?*"

"Yeah. I'm delivering that load of Swamp Virus you wanted."

Now he clearly looks startled. "Swamp Virus? I don't know . . ."

"Sure you do. In my hollow tooth." You open your mouth.

"Oh," he says with a great nod of his head. "In your tooth." He nods again. A large, hard hand comes down on your head, and you're knocked unconscious.

When you come to, you are in restraints. You're being flown through an air lock hidden in some rocks in the asteroid. Then you are dragged down a corridor and through a door which leads to a row of cages. You are thrown into one.

"Enjoy your stay," a guard says. "You won't be here long."

"What do you mean?"

"I mean you're going to help us with our experiments. We should be able to grow lots of nasty viruses on you." He laughs. "Goodbye."

The End

Two ships, one much larger than the other, are stopped near the Great Peak of Mimas. Surrounding them is a ring of six more ships. While you watch, a laser shot flashes out from the large ship and explodes a portion of the smaller ship.

"That ring of ships must be support vessels for the large command pirate ship. I wonder what they're doing with the small ship."

"There's no telling, Commander. I suggest we blast the larger ship and then hit the smaller ones. Or you could try sneaking in alone and taking over the large ship, with me here as backup—but that's fairly risky."

If you try Henry's first plan, turn to page 43.

If you try Henry's second plan, turn to page 110.

"Henry, I'm afraid that if we call a raid in we'll destroy the evidence we're looking for. I'm going to try to get in there and see firsthand what's happening."

"OK, Commander. Any ideas?"

"I've noticed that the same ships keep going in and out. We're going to waylay one on the way in, and I'm going to go aboard."

"Sounds possible. Let's get going!" Henry answers cheerfully.

It's easy to stop one of the ships and climb aboard. You find only one person there, a pilot. He seems to be there only as backup, since the ship is programmed to fly in to the mine and land on its own.

You arrest the pilot in the name of the Patrol. Then you put the pilot's space suit on and head to the mine.

The ship performs perfectly. It flies inside the asteroid and lands in a large bay filled with other ships just like it. One takes off as soon as you land. Not knowing what else to do, you leave the ship and step out onto the landing platform.

You are greeted by three space-suited figures holding laser guns on you.

"So, Arfat, we've caught you at last. We always suspected you were stealing some of the diamonds you were transporting, and now we're sure. You are off schedule by twenty minutes. Enough time to rendezvous with another ship and unload some of your cargo. Goodbye, Arfat."

You are about to tell them you are not Arfat, but you don't have time. You disappear in a flash of laser energy.

The End

"Henry, I'm willing to bet that those people are missing because they came across this secret operation and were killed," you say.

"That sounds logical, Commander."

"Let's go there and see if we can find anything."

"Roger, Commander. Here's our course."

You set the controls to follow Henry's flight plan. When you are near the spot, you disguise your ship as a mining vessel and cruise the asteroids looking for something out of the ordinary. You find nothing and decide to fly off.

"Perhaps, Commander, our presence was inhibiting a well-hidden operation from displaying any overt actions of a self-revealing nature."

"You mean maybe we've scared them into hiding. Good thought, Henry. Put us into our nondetectable mode."

Once you're invisible, you discover a number of ships entering and leaving one large asteroid.

"Henry, that looks like a mining operation to me."

"Me, too, Commander. Shall we call HQ and report our findings? An illegal mine is a good enough reason to call a raid."

"We could, Henry, but we might not find any evidence of the plot to bring war back to the solar system that way. Perhaps I should go in and try to spy on the operation."

If you decide to try spying, turn to page 102.

If you decide to try Henry's plan and call a raid, turn to page 46.

As soon as you can, you slip away after work. Quickly you put on your space suit and fly out to the pod.

The pod turns out to be a spherical structure. There are no markings on the surface except for one spot that you decide must be the door.

You approach the door and open it. A guard is standing on the other side.

"Hi, I'm bringing in . . ."

You never get to finish your sentence. The bullet passing through your space suit misses you, but it tears open a hole large enough so you die instantly from explosive decompression.

The End

"Let's try the screens, Henry. Something about that ship makes me *very* nervous, and maybe they won't notice."

But they do notice. The radio hums:

"Hello, Trader. Your defensive screens are on. We won't be able to approach close enough to help you."

You pick up the mike. "Sorry, Rescue. Must be more of a malfunction than I thought. I'll try to repair the problem."

"Roger, Trader. We'll approach as close as possible and hold there."

"Keep the screens on, Henry, until the ship is stopped. Ah! I've got an idea. Pulsate the screens. Make them look as if there really *is* a problem. But don't turn them off!"

You wait until the other ship contacts you again.

"We're in position, Trader. How are you coming with those screens?"

"I think I've finally located the problem," you radio back. "I'll have it fixed in a few seconds. Hang on.

"OK, Henry. When I give the word, I want you to cut the screens out entirely, *but bring them back to full power as fast as possible.* Got it?"

"Roger, Commander."

"OK, Henry. Do it!"

Turn to page 89.

"Roger, Commander. All systems are go."

A ship is lifting off towards you. As it gets closer, Henry reports:

"My analysis shows the ship to be of an unknown design, Commander. I don't know what to make of it."

"Yes, it does look strange, Henry. I'm not sure either. Do you think they would notice if we put up our defensive screens?"

"I don't know. Maybe we can put them on low power."

"But there's still a good chance they'd spot them?"

"Yes, Commander."

If you decide to try the defensive screens, hoping the other ship won't notice, turn to page 106.

If you decide the screens might blow your cover and you'd better just wait and see what happens, turn to page 98.

"I'm going to go down in my space suit. I think that's our only chance. Let's try another radio message first." You grab the mike and announce your plan.

No response. You sigh.

"Well, let's get on with it, Henry."

You climb into your space suit wishing you could wear your armor. But somebody would recognize it for sure if you did.

Henry cycles you out of the air lock, and you're off. You haven't gotten very far when a laser removes most of you from the physical universe.

Henry, too, is hit with laser fire. Though he's crippled, he reacts quickly enough to prevent his complete destruction. His radio is damaged, but he is able to limp away to Pluto and alert the Patrol. When they finally raid Charon, however, nobody is home. The dome is gutted, and there is no clue as to where anyone went.

As for you, the few molecules of you that were left after disintegration will eventually—after a million years or so—come to rest on Earth.

The End

You head out to the other end of the asteroid. You're not sure what you'll find or even what you're going to look for.

As you approach the end, you drop down onto the surface of the asteroid. It wouldn't do to be caught flying around. You're just in time, too. You notice a space-suited person flying toward you. You glance at the area he's coming from and catch a glimpse of an air lock just closing.

When the person is gone, you head toward the air lock, but you can't find it; all you see is rock. Suddenly you feel a vibration through your boots as a crack appears in the rocks. You duck behind a large boulder. The crack widens and out flies another space-suited figure.

A quick glance shows that the coast is clear, and you duck into the air lock before it closes.

Turn to page 112.

"Henry, I'm sneaking in, no matter how risky it is."

"Roger, Commander."

"We'll come in close to Mimas, near the Great Peak. I'll go in alone from there."

Henry drops you off at the appointed spot and waits there, ready to give you whatever aid you need. But you find you don't need anything except for the blasters in your suit. With their help you capture a group of pirates, so intent on frightening a young woman that they don't even notice you until you fire a laser blast past them.

It isn't until you get them all rounded up, however, that you learn this is a movie set and you've ruined an entire scene.

The director likes your stuff, though, and says he'll make you a star.

The End

Inside the air lock you draw your laser gun and cycle through. You find a long corridor with nobody in sight. There is a row of doors on both sides of the corridor.

You go to the closest door and open it. Inside are racks of storage shelves. Signs on the shelves read: *Venusian Swamp Virus*. But the shelves are empty. Behind the next door is another room with more storage shelves and signs. These signs say *Aldebaran Death*. The shelves are full of capsules.

You've seen enough. You close the door. Now you've got to get out of here.

You go back to the lock, cycle out, and use your jets to fly off the asteroid. When you are about two kilometers away, you call Henry on your communicator.

He turns in the alarm immediately, and soon the area is surrounded by Patrol vessels.

You discover that the plotters planned to infect visitors to their health resort with deadly diseases and then send them back to their home worlds to infect the populations there. It would have been an easy matter to continue their plotting once the disease had run its course.

At the construction site, everybody in on the scheme is captured, but you don't find anything at the Charon site. You never know if you've captured everybody—or if some have escaped to try again.

The End

At the repair facility on Luna, the technicians tell you that the work will probably take all the rest of the time you have on your tour of duty. It looks as though you're not going back into space for about six months.

Your chief is ecstatic. "We're up to our ears in paper work here. You've got a desk job now until you go on vacation."

You're not very happy—you hate paper work—but you've got no choice.

The End

You decide Henry's plan is too risky. There's no telling if you'd be able to help anybody anyway.

"Commander," Henry says suddenly, "our comm unit will still receive signals. We are only unable to *send* messages. I have a transmission coming in now."

You listen carefully to the speaker.

"SREV III, we have plotted your flight. A rescue vessel will intercept you fourteen hours from now. Repeat, fourteen hours." You groan. "We are sending another unit to help the attacked ship. At least you scared the pirates away. Over and out."

"Well, Henry, it looks as though we have a long wait." You sigh. "How about a game of space chess?" you ask reluctantly. You know you will lose. Henry always wins. You have accused him of cheating, but he denies it, smugly reminding you of human limitations.

The End

"Henry, is anybody on our line now?"

"No, sir, nobody's listening but me."

"I'm going to take a closer look at that door."

"But . . ."

"Stow it, Henry." Then you imitate the chief's gruff voice: "And that's an order!"

You program your suit computer, then head toward the door.

Turn to page 56.

"Right, Commander. We could head out and see if we run into any of the pirate activity we were warned about, or we could head in and be on hand for any trouble from the weekend rush to Venus."

If you decide to head out, turn to page 36.

If you decide to head in, turn to page 54.

At last you turn away from the display. As you do, you notice a corridor you hadn't seen before. The corridor glows bright red. You're tempted to explore it, but perhaps you should return to your ship and report to HQ first.

If you go back to the ship, turn to page 7.

If you keep searching, turn to page 23.

The large ship is engulfed in a ball of energy. It falls in on itself and is utterly consumed. You've saved the small ship and its occupants from destruction. It should be easy to capture the small pirate ships, you think.

The only problem for you—as you find out later—is that the whole setup was a movie set. You have destroyed a *very* expensive piece of stage property, not to mention a whole week's worth of shooting. Fortunately, nobody was aboard the ship you shot at, but you are in deep trouble anyway.

The End

ABOUT THE AUTHOR

JULIUS GOODMAN lives in Vermont and is a writer, editor, and designer of books. He was educated at McGill University and Emerson College.

ABOUT THE ILLUSTRATOR

RALPH REESE is a contributing artist to the *National Lampoon.* His illustrations have appeared in *Scholastic* and *The Electric Company* magazines. He has also created comic strips and features for *Crazy* and *Epic.* His first children's book was called *The First Crazy Book,* written by Byron Preiss. A former president of the Academy of Comic Book Arts, Mr. Reese has won numerous awards for his art. He has, in addition, designed animated television commercials, worked in major advertising agencies, and has taught illustration professionally.

DO YOU LOVE CHOOSE YOUR OWN ADVENTURE®?

Let your younger brothers and sisters in on the fun.

You know how great CHOOSE YOUR OWN ADVENTURE® books are to read and reread. But did you know that there are CHOOSE YOUR OWN ADVENTURE® books for younger kids too? They're just as thrilling as the CHOOSE YOUR OWN ADVENTURE® books you read and they're filled with the same kinds of decisions and different ways for the stories to end—but they're shorter with more illustrations and come in a larger, easier-to-read size.

So get your younger brothers and sisters and anyone else you know between the ages of seven and nine in on the fun by introducing them to the exciting world of CHOOSE YOUR OWN ADVENTURE®.

AV7—4/83